I Can't Wait to Never Do That Again

A glimpse into the bizarrosphere

Jeff Novotny

Image credits:

All images used by permission.

Illustrations by Makoto Okada and vectorportal.com

A note on the writing style of this book:

The reader will notice that much of the text herein does not conform to standard punctuation/capitalization/usage practices. The writing style in each paragraph is intended to reflect the inner perspective of the speaker, be it a mature observer, child, or naïf, in a rather stream-of-consciousness fashion. But as you can see, the author clearly knows how to use correct grammar and.

Interesting times at the airport today...as i got in line to board they asked what my destination was and i said i was traveling with my associate Mr. Gunn, and we have a meeting with Tara Rist, a high-powered sales rep for Bomm Manufacturing Company. We're promoting our Hi-Jack™ automobile lift. They looked at me kind of funny and asked if i had anything dangerous in my luggage. I said no but the air onboard is dry and it irritates my skin so i said i had packed Balm in my carry-on. They started getting excited because i'm sure they thought that was a good idea so then they asked if i had anything else they should know about. I remembered to bring a supply of my blood pressure medicine so i told the agent i had plenty of Drugs with me. And suddenly all the nice doggies came to meet me but before i could reach into my pocket for an unknown object the men with the shiny badges shouted at me to get down on the ground but the floor was hard and they didn't even give me a pillow. So i guess the airlines are charging for pillows now, and i asked them if there was a charge and they said yes we assure you there will be many Charges.
So then later at the hotel my cellmate introduced himself and asked if i have a girlfriend so i said no and he said well ya do now.
Next time i go to Africa i'm taking the bus!

Girl 1: What's your boyfriend's name?
Girl 2: Well, right now it's Blobby...before that I was dating a guy named Bobbly, and before that it was Bobbleby.
Girl 1: Whoa, those are really weird names...where did you meet these guys?
Girl 2: At a nightclub called Bobby L's.

Reginald was a friendly fellow and met people wherever he went, including:
Bus
Bus stop
Bus station bathroom
Bus maintenance facility hazardous materials storage area
Bus company administration building employee break room
Bus driver's Al's secret lingerie closet
Business-casual Recreational Enema Luncheon

Prank call to an online retailer:
"Yes, hello, I'm trying to use one of your promotion codes but the website isn't taking it. It's a string of letters – can I read it to you? It's B as in boy, P as in playground, C as in candy, K as in kidnap, D as in duct tape, V as in van, P as in party."

Three cheers for Medicare fraud! Hip, hip....ouch, my hip!

I tend to multitask: just the other day I was crossing the street, putting in eyedrops, talking on the phone, and getting hit by a car.

You surely won't fail to notice that this sentence is not unlike litotes.

Names for various ethnic restaurants:
Italian: Gnocchi You Up
Chinese 1: Hunan Resources
Chinese 2: Yes MSG
Vegan: Temple of Seitan
Turkish: İzdınürrediyet
Scandinavian 1: Finnish Eating
Scandinavian 2: Uwets Spojeld
Icelandic: Hakarl's Jr.
Mexican: Mixtapé
Dutch: Hieronymus Nosh
Vietnamese: Yêu Cầm Phở Mỹ Dũng
Hungarian: Megyű Vámett
Middle Eastern: Meksmi Ghasi
Indian: Nheerli Manoor
Barbecue: Habeas Porcus
American: Slopping Mall
Wing joint: J.R. EWings
Russian: If You Can Pronounce It, It's Free
British: Smith Financial Services Group Ltd.

Gen Z at work:
Boss: Good morning [Aiden/Brayden/Hayden/Jayden/
    Rayden/Zayden/etc.]
Z: How did the meeting go?
Boss: Well, you kinda had to be there.
Z: Why, what happened?

Boss: I mean, you were supposed to be there to give the presentation.
   We lost the client.
Z: We did?
Boss: Well, officially I'm afraid there is no "we" anymore.
Z: But my preferred pronouns are "we"!
Boss: Crap, now I can't even fire you.
Z: You mean fire "us".

When I have friends over, right before they leave I ask them whether they noticed the bathroom security camera.

I like to send the following text message to random numbers:
"hey could you move that window blind a little? it's blocking my view"

so the other day a man came up to me and offered to sell me something, but i didn't know what it was because he suddenly hit his head on a rock i had in my hand. then i opened my car trunk and he accidentally fell into it. he looked like he was sleeping so i thought maybe he wanted to take a nap. but i thought the trunk isn't very comfortable so maybe i should find somewhere he can sleep. so I drove out to an empty field and thought hmm this looks nice and quiet. i dragged him 50 yards into the field, out of view of the roadway (for privacy) and he is lying there asleep. i thought maybe i should cover him up so he doesn't get cold. i didn't have a blanket or anything but i remembered that earth is a good thermal insulator so i took out a shovel i bought with his credit card and shoveled some dirt on him. so i thought he would come and say thank you after he woke up but i haven't heard from him so i decided i'm not going to talk to him anymore.

While I was at work at a pharmacy, a kid came up to the counter with a box of tampons. I asked him whether he knew what they were for. He replied, "They're for my little brother. The commercial said they help you swim and ride a bike, and right now he can't do either."

Many people in the US speak Spanish nowadays. I admit I haven't studied it, though I've taken the time to learn a few useful phrases for common situations. Here's one that comes in handy: "*No sabía que ella sólo tenía trece años, Señor Juez,*" which means "I didn't know she was only 13, Your Honor."

When I was little my uncle used to sneak into my bedroom at night, slip into bed with me, place a coin under my pillow (or in my mouth) and claim to be the Tooth Fairy. But he didn't fool me...I knew he wasn't the *real* Tooth Fairy. For one thing, I could smell the cigarette smoke. And I know from past experience that the *real* Tooth Fairy smells like cigar smoke.

I've just found out that in just nine months, I'm going to be a proud father! That's right, just nine more months until my 16-year-old daughter gets out of jail.

My grandmother was kind of funny in her later years. She used to get certain words confused – for example, she would confuse "diary" with "diarrhea". So she'd say things like, "Hey Jeff, aren't you feeling well? Do you have a diary?" or "You've been in the bathroom a long time – are you having a diary in there?"
So I finally had to explain: "Look, Grandma, it's simple: a *diary* is something you write in. *Diarrhea* is something you write *with*."

I recently saw a bumper sticker that read "Abortion is not birth control". Which is true if you think about it...it's more like birth control-alt-delete.

A lot of people like to take Oreos apart when they eat them. But I don't do that because it voids the warranty.

As a fan of interesting facts and trivia, I was excited to learn a cool fact recently: the world's most common first name originates from the Middle East – it's Mohammed. And the world's most common last name originates from China – it's Wang. So I can't wait to tell my roommate about this – his name is Mohammed Wang.

I think I've finally figured out the whole birth-order phenomenon: First: birth. Then: afterbirth.

I've recently gotten into online dating; it's been going fairly well, but as you know it's quite easy to lie about your age. That happened to me recently – I found an interesting profile, and we exchanged messages and pictures, talked on the phone, and finally decided to meet. And that's when I found out.
You see, he originally said he was this many: 

But it turned out he was only this many:

I'm starting to worry that the internet will negatively affect the encyclopedia industry.

Do Not Eat Freshness Packet.

Today my landlord said he's moving me from the general population into cell block 52 because there's a rumor that someone there wants me to be his girlfriend, but he wouldn't tell me who it is. Oh boy, I like guessing games! But he said once I get into the showers I won't be guessing for long.

I'm feeling a bit ill today; I think I might have a case of indonesia. Luckily there's a new drug called Jakarta™ (indonesiumab HCl 10mg). But the package warns that you shouldn't operate any heavy machinery while taking this because you're clearly a moron.

Variation A:
Me: I had trouble getting to sleep last night.
Her: Yeah? Were you stressed about something?
Me: No, I forgot where my bed was.

———

Variation B:
At a party:
Her: Want another glass of wine?
Me: I'd better not – I had some trouble getting home last time.
Her: Really, you drank too much?
Me: No, I forgot where I live.

If you're born in Antarctica, does that mean you're Pole-ish?

my therapist recommended that i enter a residential treatment program, but i accidentally entered a Presidential treatment program. so i said hey why isn't anyone voting for me? and they said I have Electile dysfunction. and then bill clinton rolled up and said yeah i feel ur pain dude

If I correctly remember the deli scene in *When Harry Met Sally*, he was telling her about an 80's band called Klymaxx and she said no they weren't real, they were just faking it...allow me to demonstrate

Doctor: do you have any allergies?

Patient: honey

Doctor: don't call me honey

Patient: i didn't call you honey

Doctor: yes you called me at home and i'm afraid my wife will find out
about us

Patient: ok honey

Doctor: now, are you ready for your colon exam?

Patient: umm...but you're an optometrist

Doctor: yeah, but for you i'll make an exception ☺

Patient: this isn't the kind of playing dress-up i had in mind, uncle
melvin

If there were an organized crime ring in the Middle East, would it be
called the Maffiyah?

Dang, I was gonna bring sexy back but I put it in the wrong gear and it
went forward instead.
Sorry, bakery window!

A good name for a repo agency would be Little Seizer's.

Help! I've been kidnapped by militant vegans – they held me at
asparagus spearpoint and took me to their secret compound,
Granolistan.

1: Hey, I have an idea.

2: Oh, what is it?

1: I didn't mean right *now* – just occasionally I'll have some kind of
   idea. I didn't say I'm *having* an idea.

Well, it appears my future as an inventor is in serious doubt. To date,
no manufacturers are interested in my Poison Ivy/Sandpaper Bra.
Time for plan B: Pizza Rental!

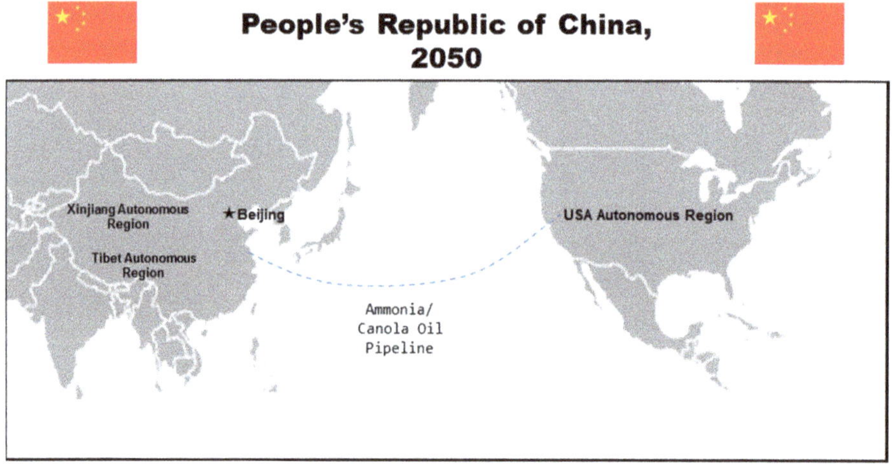

When I went trick-or-treating I found a sliver of metal in my chocolate bar so I went to the guy's house who gave it to me and he said it's called a shank, and he showed me how to use it in both stabbing and slashing methods.
I thought I'd been tricked, but this was a treat!

Guy 1: My therapist says I might be having a "midlife crisis." What is that?
Guy 2: What? I can't hear you over that Corvette engine! And who's that girl in the back seat?
Guy 1: Which one?

Police report that there has been a suspicious-looking individual lurking around the local playground named Alec M. Young.

Someone tried to tell me you can make a pie out of pumpkins. But that's nonsense because pumpkins are just Halloween decorations. If you're going to eat decorations, you might as well try to eat a candy cane, Easter egg, or snowman's nose! Actually, I tried eating a snowman's nose once but the snowman said yo hold up bro, i ain't into that kinky stuff.

I was looking for a primary-care physician (PCP) in my insurance network, so I searched for "where can I find PCP," whereupon Google

responded with a warning about the danger of using PCP and a list of places to get help.
Good eye, Google, but these places aren't in my network.
Next time I should search for "where to find cheap PCP".

As per my understanding of the metric system, there are 1000 graham crackers in a kilograham?

Seen on a job application:
Current position: _Emergency Dispatcher_
Work phone #: _911_

They say you can't milk a dead horse. But that's not gonna stop me from trying!

Mechanic: Hello, what brings you in today?
Customer: For some reason, whenever I drive to the playground my van gets 30 pounds heavier.

Dinner at the Icelandic restaurant was going quite well until my entree ransacked my fishing village and ran off with my daughter.

What would be a good Christmas gift for someone named Nottie R. Nyce?

Dec. 23:
Customer: Where can I find Christmas cards?
Employee: Umm...like two weeks ago.

Woohoo, I'm looking forward to the upcoming Super Cup – gonna watch those girls score plenty of runs by kicking the puck into the basket and finishing 5 under par.

Jerry Springer: Darth, when it comes to 25-year-old Luke....you ARE the father!
Luke: Nooooo!

Smurf...Smurves?

Dang, I dropped my hot dog and it rolled behind the toilet. 5-second rule! (actually, 5.9 seconds according to the surveillance camera, which was recently calibrated)

Why do people say "The problem is, is..."? Isn't one "is" is enough?

Hmm, I can't decide whether to join AA or AAA.

I saw this sign today. As a non-lactator, what would happen if I were to enter this room? Would it be like the scene from Superman where he gets neutralized in the molecule chamber? They might make me kneel before Zod.

My owner is requiring me to go to the next AA meeting wearing only a coating of strawberry jam. But I much prefer raspberry jam. So I'll probably file a religious-discrimination lawsuit because I'm a Raspbyterian.

Ever have someone ask you about a person with the same last name, "Any relation?" Next time that happens I'm going to say, "Nope, I've never had relations with them."

Good news – I got a call from the IRS saying that they owe me a big refund and all I have to do is send some Amazon gift cards to an anonymous P.O. box somewhere in Mexico. I'm sure it's real because the caller had a foreign accent which means they're Sophisticated.

Heads up, folks – this season's harvest might not be quite as bountiful as it should be; it turns out *someone* forgot to do the human sacrifice last week.
Isn't that right, Larry?

So this guy named Marty Poppins showed up at my door and said hey, can i borrow your kids.

Woohoo – I've been recognized at work. Apparently there was an unknown individual wandering around and peeking into the ladies' restrooms, and my coworker was walking around with the security guard when she suddenly pointed me out and said "That's him! I recognize his creepy grin and shifty eyes!"
It's great to be recognized for all you do, even when you think people don't notice you because you're on the ceiling.

So Grandma went to her weekly ~~Bingo game~~ rap battle, which is where she ~~talks~~ smokes with her ~~friends~~ homies from ~~church~~ cell block D. I can almost hear the sweet sounds of ~~Lawrence Welk~~ N.W.A. coming from her ~~Escalade~~ Toyota Tercel.

Oops, I've been caught sholpifting. Pifting the shols, as they say.

Today the new neighbor from Australia came to my door and said "Oima six offinda." And everyone was scrambling to take their kids inside, probably because he'd already met their kids.

Shootings at schools, shootings at workplaces...but why are there never any shootings at Target? These shooters aren't very good at following directions. It's a wonder they ever hit anything.

Binoculars: you'll never look at your neighbors the same way again.

Around this festive time of year, Santa's elves are busy making phones, computers, and such...I've seen pictures of them and they're like 8 years old and they live in China!

Apparently the local police department is having a contest – if you can steal a car you win a pair of handcuffs.

When the Chinese take over, I predict that Shea Stadium will be renamed Hsieh Stadium.

A favorable thing to say on a first date is: "What good timing – tomorrow I'm taking my monthly shower."

I'd like to create a diet version of Milk Duds called Water Duds.

Remember, life is like a box of chocolates: it's what the creepy neighbor uses to lure you into his van.

I got paid today. 90% of it I'll save, the other half I'll use for math tutoring.

Remember – hugs, not drugs.
.

.

.

Okay, now drugs.

I was rather disappointed today that no one noticed my emotional-support tapeworm.
Sorry, Clyde!

During a presentation today my boss told me to wrap it up. But instead
I started to rap it up. So she said wow those are some phat rhymes. I
don't know what that means but am I getting a raise?

1: See you later, alligator
2: After awhile, pedophile
1: Wait, that's not how it –
2: Get back in the van, Timmy

Getting pregnant while feeling sick is ill-conceived.

I hope I don't get into a bar fight at church again.

Oops, I made a little mistake today at the petting zoo – I thought it was
a tasting zoo.

So it appears you can go to school for nursing now? How hard can it
be...just attach the baby and away you go!

I sure hope I don't drive off without my car keys, or I might get
stranded somewhere not knowing how I got there.

It's fun to go to the beach because you can P in the C.

This car ad says it has heated seats and a rear defroster. Aren't they the same thing?

I've spent far too much time today trying to determine the difference between a flume and a spume.

Today at school, Harry and Ron wouldn't play with me because I'm a Muggle. Then they cast a spell on me called Impotens Incontinentis Permanentia. So now I'm having a little, you know, "trouble".

At the MRI scanner:
Technician: Are you wearing anything made of metal?
Terminator T-1000: Umm...yeah, about that...

Note to self: Sid's Daycare isn't the best naming choice.

Here's a neat trick: you can read 62 different diet books all at once, just by reading the following sentence: Don't eat processed food.
You're welcome!

Now that they are no longer performing, do you think Hall & Oates are haulin' oats?

Today I saw an advertisement for "Accident Attorneys". This is probably someone who intended to go to medical school but accidentally went to law school instead. They probably went to Bob's Discount Law School & Dry Cleaners.

Customer service: Your call is important to us.
Me: Oh, you probably say that to all the guys.
....don't lie to me, Kyssandra

I read an interesting quote about foxes: "Foxes run cat software on dog hardware."

Has anyone bothered to ask the yoga mat whether he prefers to be called yoga Mathew?

How can you be "very pregnant" but not "slightly pregnant"?

If I were to start a religion, I'd call it Mr. Church.

If you'd care to know how my last date went, here's a brief snippet:
Me: It's nice to meet you.
Her: The pleasure is mine.
Me: Um, no, it's mine.

Her: It's mine, give it back!
Me: Stop it!
Her: Mom!

At work today after I botched my team's presentation, my coworker looked at me with annoyance and exclaimed, "You ruined everything!" So apparently my All-Purpose Ruiner is working much better now that I've replaced the batteries.

At the rehab therapist:
Therapist: I hope you haven't been using again.
Patient: well i gotta admit yeah i've been using
Therapist: *(groans)* OK, fine – what have you been using?
Patient: well off the tee usually i'd use a driver, or maybe a 3-wood if it's a short par-4. or if i'm adjusting air brakes then i'd use a type 2 torque wrench with 6" extension shaft.
Therapist: Interesting...go on.
Patient: but out in your parking lot i usually use methamphetamine or maybe crack and did you know in french it's called *le craque.*
Therapist: Who is selling this stuff to you?
Patient: well you probably don't know him
Therapist: Why not?
Patient: because he's your dad
Therapist: Oooooh, sick burn bro

One of my friends just invited me to a swingers' event. That sounds like fun because I like baseball and golf, both of which involve a lot of swinging. Maybe someone will give me some pointers.
(Later): THAT WAS NOT WHAT I EXPECTED.

Good news: the plural of golf is golves.
But not gloves – that's the plural of glof.

Today the customer service agent asked if I'd like to participate in a brief survey. What on earth could they need to know about my briefs? I already told them I'm wearing the Barney the Dinosaur pair this week (and next week).

Paradoxical irony: Stigler's Law of Eponymy[1]

Today I baked some German-style Christmas bread, but it was stollen.

I forgot to take my birth control today so I started birthing and couldn't stop! And then someone tried to give birth to me but I gave it back because I'd already had enough births.

---

[1] This law says that a scientific discovery is generally not named after the person who first discovers it. As can be predicted, this fact was not discovered by Stigler.

Um...what should I do if I've accidentally eaten my young? (besides producing less delicious-looking offspring next time)

I think it's interesting that there's an American politician named Kirstjen Nielsen....imagine going to Sweden and finding someone named Bob Smith. Only he pronounces it "Bobe Smeet."

Hmm, apparently these guys Roe and Wade don't get along – they've been fighting since 1973. Why doesn't one of them say to the other, "OK dude, I'm gonna let you win but you have to tell everyone I won." Problem solved!

If I were to open a grocery store, it would be called Gross Restore.

There's an insurance company called State Farm – that reminds me of China in the 1950's.

Interesting viewpoint: taking out a loan is like renting money.

Tip for students: if you can't find your way to math class, just take the square route.

If a crop disease destroyed the grain used for whiskey-making, would it be called the Bourbonic Plague?

Interesting fact: according to Google, you can open a maximum of 9,000 tabs in Chrome simultaneously.
(Reply from friend): "I'm at 9010...9011...9012..."

Today in a parking lot I saw a sign which read "Do not leave children in a hot car." So I found an old boring car and left them in there instead.

A good slogan for a retail store would be: "Everything you need...until you need it."

Woman 1: I just found out I'm pregnant.
Woman 2: Congratulations – do you know the baby's sex?
Woman 1: What, he's having sex already? I knew I shouldn't have let those girls in there.

And now, a haiku:
<blockquote>
Pool cleaning guy's here!
He just went upstairs with Mom.
We don't have a pool.
</blockquote>

I was supposed to meet with my autobiographer today, but I waited for a long time and she never showed up! So I fired her.

Time for a nice cup of tea. Today's selection: Obscenitea. It's both refreshing *and* inappropriate.
Now, where the $*!)#&% is that teabag?

(Sigh) Great, now I've gotta build an extension onto my Barbie house – the Barbies have been bugging me to do it so they can open a "massage parlor".

When I eat doughnuts, I usually don't eat the dough part, just the nut.

They say the dirtiest thing in a hotel room is the TV remote control. But I've been watching the remote for the last half-hour and it hasn't done anything remotely dirty.
Dang, I thought I was going to get some free adult entertainment.

A suitable name for a librarian would be Page Reade.

Today I got a call from the state police saying that the person posing as my doctor is a known individual operating without a medical license. Silly guy – it's not even Halloween yet and he's wearing a doctor costume!

At the time when I was applying to colleges, someone asked whether I'd applied to any safety schools. In fact, I'd applied to the Fire Safety Institute in Podunk, Iowa. But it's a good thing I didn't go there because the school eventually burned down.

Today I saw a sign that said BLOOD DRIVE and you probably need a license to drive one of those. But where would you drive it?

If there were a word to describe a patio, it would be: patious.

I must admit that I'm not that confident in the bedroom.
I am, however, quite confident in the bathroom.

Woman 1: I just found out I'm pregnant.
Woman 2: Congratulations! Do you know the sex?
Woman 1: Of course I know the Sex – how do you think I made the
          baby in the first place?

From the little I know about Spanish, it seems a mosquito is a small mosque?

Today at the supermarket I heard a lady in the next aisle say "Gotta go, I have to change Kevin's diaper." So I called across the aisle, "Ooh, change mine too!"

New Year's resolution: I'm going to spend far less time trying to believe that it's not butter. This cannot be achieved (it says so on the package).

I keep seeing the word "love" everywhere and I think it's probably the plural of "loaf".

today i went to the zoo and accidentally fell into the chimpanzee exhibit. but the chimpanzees were very nice and used my preferred pronouns and even gave me some of their marijuana. i was like whoa where did you get this, did one of the visitors drop it? and they said no it's an employment benefit we get from our union. and so i said wow are you guys hiring? and they said well generally they try to laterally promote existing employees and in fact there are several lemurs vying for the open position right now but we'll take your information.
...And that, Officer, is how the drugs got into my pants.

Hey folks, if anyone needs a web designer...hire a spider.

Today I went on a fact-finding mission and found some facts! I know they were facts because they came from a fax machine, which is where fax come from.

Woohoo, my secret admirer gave me a mixtape. It included duct tape, videotape, and tapestry, which means now I can redecorate my tapeworm enclosure.

I hear that North Korea has deployed a new offensive missile.
Apparently this missile makes rude comments about your weight,
causing the enemy forces to retreat in embarrassment.
Victory!

I recently spotted a cookbook called *Vegan Finger Foods*, but I don't
think fingers are vegan.

My South American neighbors were talking rather loudly, and I heard
them talking about something called S.E.M., but I had no idea what
that was. Then I figured out they wanted to try S y M.
But probably not while the grandkids are visiting.

Why do obituaries list the cause of death, but never the cause of birth?

Soy Sauce.
Hola Sauce, soy Milk.
Hola Milk, soy Cheese.
Milk: *¡No soy tu padre – no estas queso reál!*

So we know that Frosty the Snowman went down to the village with a
broomstick in his hand. What the song doesn't say is what he did to
those poor villagers with that broomstick. And he dared us to catch
him.

A peculiar concept, this Hamburger Helper. Usually hamburgers are the ones helping *me* (with bathing and other activities).

Traveler: I'd like to buy a ticket to Nisneyland.
Ticket agent: It's pronounced New Zealand.

I saw an older lady browsing in the girls' toy aisle, when she asked the clerk, "Excuse me, where are your boy toys?"
So I said, "I'm right here, ma'am."

I'm afraid to go to sleep now because the Christmas song said "he seize you while you're sleeping" and I don't want *that* happening again.

The sign in the restroom said "Employees must wash hands". So I waited for an employee to come and wash my hands, but no one showed up. So I thought, well, I'd better not attempt to do it myself.

If Darth Vader had a sister, her name would be Ella, and she'd use the Force to lift and lower things to various floors.

Hmm, the crossword puzzle clue is "two-wheeled vehicle". I think it's probably "defective tricycle".

Ceci n'est pas une perceuse.

Today a coworker offered to show me pictures of her dog, and I said no thanks, and she said oh, are you a cat person? And I asked what do I look like, some kind of cat-human hybrid? And she said no, not exactly. So it looks like I'm going to need a new makeup artist.

today i was pecking at some free birdseed someone had left in the roadway when suddenly an anvil dropped onto my head.

I've heard that baked is healthier than fried. As a result, I'm currently baked.

Therapist: So, do you often eat out of boredom?
Patient: No, I usually eat right out of the container.
The sign on the water fountain said "Closed For Sanitary Purposes".
That's OK – I was planning to use it for unsanitary purposes.

Today I learned that a pamphlet is simply a smaller version of a pamph.

My employer decided to reserve a section of the office to use for the interns to complete a training course. So that means it will be a Sectional Intern Course.

I like Oreos, but I don't take them apart because it voids the warranty.

Restrooms are for when you didn't stroom enough the first time.

Animal cracker? That doesn't sound like a very pleasant job.

Waiter: What would you like to drink?
Customer: I'll try the Mountain Dew.
Waiter: No...Dew or Dew not – there is no try.

I keep getting ads in the mail for both cosmetics and AARP. So some marketing research has apparently designated me as a sassy senior. I was so surprised I almost spit my prune juice all over my designer shoes. I used to play foosball but had to quit because I injured my foos.

I saw mommy kissing Santa Claus! I knew it was him because he was delivering presents, but he was disguised as a mailman for some reason. And he even had red hair just like mine!

It's tons of fun to go on vacation, except in Europe – then it's metric tons of fun.

Whoopsie – I accidentally threw out the baby with the bathwater. I later discovered my mistake when some wastewater technicians came by and offered to sell me a baby.

I can't afford a car right now, so instead I'm learning how to drive a stick.

I hate it when Yoda says "your weapons, you will not need them," and then I end up needing them. But you know what they say – it's better to have it and not need it than have it and think you need it but not know you have it and go back to get it and realize you had it all along and then find out you never really needed it in the first place.

I'm going to start making homemade soda, so I'd better study up on Fizzics.

Hugh Downs and Barbara Walters just announced that it's 20/20. So that saves me a trip to the optometrist.

I'm learning how to tell time: on weekdays I tell it to go faster. On weekends I tell it to go slower.

A bird's first day out of the nest:

 "I'm gonna fly like an eagle, into the....furniture"

Me: Do you take debit?
Cashier: Yes.
Me: That's good. I take Debbie.

When someone offers to sell me Girl Scout cookies, I smile creepily and ask, "Do you have any Boy Scouts?"
They usually don't have any Boy Scouts.

Customer service rep: What state do you live in?
Me: Confusion. But I spend January to March in Despair.

Advice to a young axe murderer: Don't just kill the first person you see; be sure to chop around.
I'm going to go around and put labels on things that say "Danger: Do not touch!" in braille.

Well...I found myself caught amidst a love triangle. But later on I learned that it was more of a love octagon.

If I were to open a philosophy bookstore, it would be called Kant Stop.

Yech...this deodorant-flavored ice cream tastes like soap.

Have you ever woken up too early, thinking it was time to get up for the day? I did that and started scampering around to store acorns for winter but then looked at the calendar and realized it was only April.

Today I made two mistakes, the second of which was making a third mistake.

I heard about this place called the Olive Garden, which apparently has a garden full of olives and you can go and eat the olives but if the owners catch you they'll throw you into the Erotic Dungeon.

Today my car ran out of gas, so I tried using Girl Power to get it to run. But that didn't work because the girls weren't strong enough to push it up the hill. Next time I'll try Horse Power.

It's too bad I'm not allowed to talk to strangers – they're the only ones who offer me candy.

today on the school bus someone tried to steal my *Frozen* lunchbox so i said hey Let It Go but he wouldn't so i swung it and whacked him over the head and fortunately it was *Frozen* solid so it knocked him unconscious. then i took his Dukes of Hazzard lunchbox and the bus driver saw me with it and said hey did you whack that kid and i said no, them Duke boys come and done it. and he said yeah they were in here last week looking for cigarettes.

Getting into a relationship with someone much older: Carbon Dating
Getting into a relationship with someone much older, hoping they'll die and leave you their money: Expiration Dating

Well, I suppose it's time to stop playing with dolls, and start playing with dowels.

It's not a hostage situation; it's "forced hospitality".

Today I decided to have lunch at Yung's Asian Grill, but instead the GPS directed me to Young Asian Girl. So I walked in and said to the (very) young lady behind the counter, I'd like to order the Hot Yung Fun special for two, extra spicy. And she says ok, come with me to back room.

I built a gingerbread house and put a gingerbread man in it but now he's complaining the hallways aren't wide enough and there's no accessible ramp so he's threatening to report me to gingerbread OSHA. But it turns out that he doesn't talk so much once you bite off his arms. Oh, and if you want to eat a gingerbread house, remember not to eat the bathrooms.

A cheerful holiday thought: it's OK to like gingerbread men, but if you prefer gingerbread boys you might have to answer to the local authorities.

So apparently in Mexico the three genders are male, female, and tamale?

If anyone sees Oscar the Grouch, tell him I want my $300 by Tuesday or I'm gonna trash his place.

If you're a retrovirus, every day is like Halloween! Except that it's more of a reverse Halloween, since you're forcing everyone else to dress up as you.

It's a good thing Halloween is over – I was having trouble finding the fine line between trick-or-treating and breaking-and-entering.

I think it's time to lay off the ginger snaps and switch to ginger schnapps.

Sign on restroom wall:

Your restroom visit will be recorded to ensure ~~your~~ MY satisfaction

I've hired a law firm, but they seem to procrastinate quite a bit. So maybe I should put off paying this bill from Duitt Tomaro & Waite. I like the Pittsburgh Steelers because their name is a combination of "steel" and "walrus": *Le walrus d'acier s'étouffe avec le futbol.*

Now that Halloween is over, it's time for some reverse trick-or-treating: I'll go to people's houses and give *them* poisoned candy.

1: I'm on a bit of an adventurous streak as far as my food choices – last night I decided to try suckling pig.

2: Mmm, I've heard that's really good.

1: Yeah, I've never suckled a pig before.

2: So how was the pig?

1: It sucked.

For lunch today I was going to have some honey-glazed ham, but I'm a vegan so I can't eat honey.

I recently learned that if you want to remember something, you have to dismember it first. For example, today I was trying to remember where I'd put my hatchet, which of course reminds me of the French term for ground beef, *viande haché*,[2] so I absentmindedly wandered over to the old abandoned refrigerator...and discovered lil' Timmy was still in there! And eww, he's still wearing the same clothes as he was last week! Now, if only there were a way to remember where I put that hatchet.

I've decided to stop playing golf, which of course means that now I'll have to *start* playing golf.

At a casino I saw a window labeled "Bill Breaking". Presumably that's where they take ducks who can't pay their gambling debts and offer a little "encouragement". But why make it so obvious? They should label it "Free Breadcrumbs" instead.

---

[2] I actually prefer the German word, *Hackfleisch*. More descriptive, don't you think?

Today I heard on the radio, all the single ladies put your hands up, so I put my hands up. And the surgeon said umm...you're not supposed to be awake right now. And you won't be a lady for a few more minutes.

What should I have for breakfast, eggs or doughnuts? Oh well, I suppose it dozen matter.

I think I'm going to start betting on football. First, I bet Americans will call it soccer.

Woohoo, I have a date with someone from Craigslist...her ad said she likes a generou$$$ man who'll bring her lots of flower$$$. I asked her what kind of flowers she likes and she said mainly 50's and 100's. I've never heard of that kind so I'm just going to give her some money and she can buy her own flowers.

Do inconvenience stores have insecurity cameras?

Recently I was looking for a recipe for Red Velvet Cake but my computer auto-corrected Velvet to Vervet so I ended up getting the wrong ingredients. So I've discovered I don't really like Red Vervet Cake. And now I'm banned from the zoo.

Variation A:
When life gives you lemons, start throwing them at someone until they buy you some lemonade.

~~~~~

Variation B:
When life gives you lemons: 3D-printed cornbread octopus!

Today someone gave me a Bad Touch so I yelled Stranger Danger and then the nurse came running in and said um so do you want to cancel your colonoscopy?

If you were caught burglarizing the Flintstones' house, you'd probably have to yabba dabba do time.

Woohoo, I just found a $20 bill! Whoever lives here should be more careful about locking their doors and windows.

The other day I saw a self-driving car going through a fast-food drive-thru. Maybe it was on its lunch break?

A flyer came in the mail advertising a sale with the text "URGENT BLOWOUT", and I couldn't help thinking that it sounded like a euphemism for diarrhea.
~~~~~

Ouch – a tractor-trailer kicked up a stone and inflicted 2d8 of damage to my windshield. And I couldn't even cast a deflection spell because it's prohibited by a local ordinance.

Tonight I'm hanging out with my friends Ashley, Ashlee, and Ashleigh. Later we're going to meet up with Lindsay, Lindsey, Lynzi, and Lyndzee.

I woke up groggy and I'm not quite sure where I am, but it looks like R. Kelly's hotel room. Fortunately I know what to do in this situation: stay calm and try not to act like a 14-year-old girl.

As they say, actions speak louder than words. Which is why shouting is an action.

I'm trying to teach a cow to speak French, but the only word it can say is "méux", so I said sacre bleu Bessie, are you ever going to learn this, and the cow said hey my name's Aurélie, and I said EN FRANÇAIS and then it blasted me with 2 kg of le mànûre because in France they use the metric system.

today's dilemma: uncle Stu says he'll give me some candy if i'm a good boy. but then i heard him tell aunt Myrna he's decided he's into bad boys so he isn't going to live with her any more. so am i supposed to be a good boy or a bad boy?

Oh no, the quail ate my petunias! Time to start planting Toxic Petunia, which also happens to be my superhero name.

If it ain't broke, don't ___________.
a) break it
b) fix it
c) claim it's broken and then try to return it and the clerk says um just because you attached a propeller to this watermelon doesn't mean it can fly and btw that's a nice dress you're wearing and i say thanks i made it out of taped-together paper bags and did you know they still make paper bags.

On Halloween I was dressed as a giant carrot and some people said to me hey nice costume and I was like what costume?
Not wanting to drive through an intersection that was photo-enforced, I instead took a slight detour and went through one that was coloring book-enforced.

I'm beginning to suspect that my mind is trying to follow my body around.

Officer: Good afternoon...do you know how fast you were going?
Google Self-Driving Car: Yes – exactly 68.2 mph.
Officer: I'm going to have to issue you a citation for exceeding the speed limit.

Google Self-Driving Car: Sending your internet search history to your
wife. Found 62 instances of 'how to hide sexy sheep pics from
my girlfriend'. Proceed with citation?
Officer: Have a nice day, Mr. Google...move along now....

I'm finding it rather difficult to be a parent, primarily because I don't
have any children.

Sign outside prison: Violators will be prosecuted
Sign inside prison: Prosecutors will be violated

From what the police are telling me, apparently this isn't one of those
clothing-optional post offices.

I set a trap for the Avon salesperson who always comes to my door:
when she rings the bell she'll fall into a 6'x8' hole filled with
mosquitoes, so hopefully she'll have her Avon mosquito repellent
handy. Then I'll offer to sell her a ladder, and a great opportunity to
become a ladder distributor herself.

It would be funny to see a Cialis commercial where James Brown shows
up in people's bedrooms singing "Get On Up".

I hope my ancestors start walking upright soon – my back is starting to ache.

People keep telling me I have Capgras syndrome, but there's no way I'm believing those fakers.

At the store I saw a magazine called Cosmopolitan, which is apparently about bioengineering, since it promises to tell you how to create a bed-shaking organism. And apparently this organism can fly, since it says it will "send your man into the stratosphere". Ahh, the wonders of biotechnology.

How can the multiverse theory be true if I'm confident that in at least one universe I figured out how to collapse the multiverse?

I've got to cut back on costs – time to stop going to the dollar store and switch to the 99¢ store.

So I tried to party like it's $19.99, but I couldn't quite afford that so I tried to party like it was only $11.99, but that didn't work out either because there were no cars or electricity back then, plus I don't really like mead.

Nurse: Doctor, where is the patient who was in this room earlier?

Doctor (*grimly*): I'm afraid we lost him.

Nurse: But...he just had a broken ankle!

Doctor: Aha – that means he couldn't have gotten very far.

OK, I'll finally admit it – I've developed an addiction to prescription sunglasses.

I don't very much like the term "tater tots" – I prefer "potato children".

I'm thinking of moving out of my bouncy house and moving up to a bouncy castle.

This is the email address I want; just imagine dictating it to someone: all_oneword_lowercase_underscore.net@dotnetdotcom.org

Hey, I saw something! But only when woodworking.

A while back I greeted the cashier at a McDonald's and asked how he was doing. He said, "Not too good – I'm middle-aged, overweight, and working at McDonald's."

Overheard exchange between mother and child:
Mother: Look, piggies!
Child: I hate piggies.
Mother: You hate everything.
Child: Yes I do!

I heard on the news that 50-odd people were shot in Chicago over the weekend. At least they were odd people – leave the normal people alone.

While in a class teaching English overseas, I asked the students, "All right, who can tell us what a thermometer is?"
A young student raised her hand and answered, "It is what you stick in the ass of the dog."

I'm impressed – I was on hold during a conference call, and they were playing a country song about being on hold during a conference call.

I remember a certain video game from back in the 90's which read the time from your computer, and if you played it on a Friday night it chided you for being a loser.

Guy 1: I was chatting online with this girl, and all of a sudden she disappeared and I never heard back from her. What do you think happened?
Guy 2: Maybe his mother took away his internet privileges.

Actual online wine review, ca. 2007:
Have you people lost your minds? This stuff is swill. It makes Yellow Tail look like an '82 Bordeaux. $3 a bottle for the Cab and Merlot. The appellation is "America." That would be like saying a wine is from Europe. Have you no concept of climate, terroir etc. This crap is fermented in rusty tanks with dead animals I presume. Possibly in a dumpster somewhere in south Fresno.

Overheard in a grocery store:
Child: Mom, can we get this?
Mother: The problem is, you're the only one who'll eat it.
Child: That's not a problem.

If I were to start a retail business, the slogan would be "We eliminate the middleman...and make it look like an accident!"

The only reason I drink beer is because I can't eat it.

Have you ever noticed that you can never find a needle when you need one, but sure enough, as soon as you start rooting around in a haystack to find the body you stashed in there...ouch!

As the saying goes, when the cat's away, the mice will play. But what if the mice want to play with the cat? In that case they will have to fashion an ersatz cat-like object out of straw, fabric, and meat scraps.
Anyone know how can I check a $12 bill to see whether it's real?

My doctor said I have an iron deficiency, so I should take a supplement. But I didn't know which one to get, so I got a curling iron, a waffle iron, and a tire iron. The store clerk wanted to know if I'd be cooking, cross-dressing, or mugging. So I said yep, just a typical Friday night.

Experience shows that Russian Roulette is perfectly safe for five out of six people.

The other day I was making a tasty grilled cheese sandwich with bacon. But I absentmindedly forgot to cook the bacon before putting it onto the sandwich. So, instead of throwing the whole thing away and starting over, I simply put the slices of bread in the dishwasher, then stepped away to renew my subscription to *Captain Kangaroo vs. Dyspeptic Chimp*[3]. But after the wash cycle was complete I discovered that the bread had mysteriously disappeared! Which left only one possibility: someone had surreptitiously absconded with it after sedating me with methohexital/acepromazine. Thereupon I telegraphed the local constabulary, who rode up prepared with a battery of questions, including how could you be so stupid, and why don't you put some pants on while we're here.

As every doctor knows, if you can't helium or curium, you'll have to barium.

I aim to have a goal someday...

My kids are always getting into things and taking them apart...while I was napping, my 6-year-old just disassembled my pacemaker.

---

[3] *le Chimpanzé Dyspepsique*

A nutritionist told me that eating differently colored foods helps to ensure varied nutrition. So this Froot Loops and Marshmallow Peeps casserole should be healthy indeed!

Message from my computer:
"To check for updates, you must install an update for Windows Update."
Glad I've been updated.

The ad claims that Oreo is milk's favorite cookie. Has anyone bothered to ask milk its opinion? I have. (This is not the first conversation I've had with milk.)

Why do I always forget that Baseline doesn't rhyme with Vaseline?

Today I had a bit of a stomach ache, and I read that a possible cause could be Pregnancy, and if you have Pregnancy you should take prenatal vitamins. Maybe these will help.

♪ "I'm just burnin', doin' the Neutron Dance..."
(*Later*): My doctor has informed me that the burnin' is not related to the Neutron Dance.

I was going to take the Highway to the Danger Zone. But it was closed, so I had to take the bus through a rather rough neighborhood. So I suppose it worked out to be the same thing.

Him: You know, I've decided that I'm kind of like a goat.
Her: Really...in what way?
Him: Just in general.

I'm thinking of changing my body temperature; getting tired of the ol' 98.6. Any suggestions?

If TV signals from Earth are reaching another planet, we're wasting money. Powering a transmitter is expensive, and beings on another planet aren't buying the products in the TV commercials that pay the power bill.

If I were to invent a medicine for erectile dysfunction, I'd call it Peptoc™.

I was thinking of making some homemade pretzels, but it turns out I might knot knead them.

Interesting fact: Patent GB1426698 was filed by Arthur Pedrick for a "Photon Push-Pull Radiation Detector For Use in Chromatically Selective Cat Flap Control And 1000 Megaton Earth-Orbital Peace-Keeping Bomb".

There's chaos in my kitchen! The English muffins are fighting the French toast over control of the German chocolate cake. If they don't stop it I'm going to throw them all into the Dutch oven.

Alert: Your computer has been infected by the Honor System virus. Please forward this message to everyone you know, then delete all the files on your hard drive. Thank you for your cooperation.

I think I'm going to change my policy on taking candy from strangers. Now it will be: Don't *forcibly* take candy from strangers. Unless it's really good candy.

Really, Mr. Pharmacist, this embarrassing prescription is for...my significant other(s).

I for one get the feeling Charles is no longer in charge.

Variation A:

Today I went to the Grammar Doctor. I was using my active voice, so he had to put me into a comma, whereupon he administered a semicolonoscopy. This was bracketed by an awkward period of silence, though that's subjective, predicated on your definition of awkward. But don't quote me on that (parenthetically).

~~~~~~

Variation B:

Doctor: Hello, thanks for being on time for your appointment.

Patient: No problem – I was feeling punctuational today.

Doctor: You mean punctual?

Patient: No, punctuational. Let me explain: Last night I had a date with an English teacher. We started doing the comma sutra, and right at the point of exclamation, she pulls out a caret! So now there's a quote-unquote 'period' coming from my colon, so I dashed in to see you.

Doctor (seeing dollar signs): Hmm, that could underscore a greater issue which, parenthetically, could equal a week in the hospital, full stop. Question, Mark?

Mark the Intern: No questions, Dr. Pilcrow.

(*yawn*) I think I just saw the Boring Aurorealis.

Hmm, I can't remember whether I've forgotten this before...
~~~~~~

No more ballroom dance classes for me – this lame instructor doesn't even know how to do the Truffle Shuffle. That's OK – I'm switching to hip-hop aerobics. That way I'll get thinner and phatter at the same time.

I was going to go off on a tangent, but I got distracted and ended up going off on a different tangent.

I think it's time to drop the Crouton Bomb.

Yes, but is it medical-grade peanut butter?

Sorry, but "male" is already taken. Please choose another gender(s).

I'm taking probiotics and antibiotics at the same time to see which one wins.

I feel like cooking something...should I go for a wok or take a leek?

I've been losing a lot of money lately by reverse-pickpocketing. You really have to watch your wallet these days!

I think it's time to be put into a medically induced comb-over, or something.

Today I found out that my company has a Public Relations department. But I thought having relations in public was against the law, according to this ankle-monitoring device I have to wear.

At a New Year's Eve party I tried to kiss someone under the mistletoe. But then his mother came running up and yelled what are you doing, he's only five! So I said wow, he looks even younger. ; –)

Really, I was planning to go to my bulimia support group, but something came up.

To commemorate Valentine's Day, I'm writing a story entitled "15 Shades of Gray". It's about a bored homemaker who meets a mysterious stranger who paints her gray and teaches her to swim like a trained dolphin. She learns to jump through hoops, balance a beach ball on her snout, and even say simple phrases like "So, buddy, what are you in for?"

In my medicine cabinet I have some ipecac syrup, but it's expired; I'm afraid if I take it, it might...not?...make me throw up.

You know, some days it's so hot you can barely keep the ice cream in your underwear from melting.

I invited my friend over to watch football, but he mistakenly went to some random house on Crackhead Ave. instead of my address on Crackhead Blvd., so now he's nowhere near here. And I'm not getting mixed up with people from THAT part of town.

Newspaper headline:

Hurricane DeShawn Pounds US Virgin Islands
Islands say they expected their first time to be better

The area where Washington, D.C., now stands was originally a mosquito-infested swamp. It took years to drain and clear the land before our nation's government was moved to the city in 1800. Apparently, not much has changed.

If there's one thing I've learned, it's that I should have learned more than one thing.

I rented this strange-looking movie which oddly didn't have a description, and no recognizable actors. It's called *DVD Lens Cleaner*. I can't be sure, but I think it's a documentary about the brave men and women who sneak into our bedrooms at night and clean our DVD lenses...and then try on our underwear.

I saw a magazine cover that said *Reverse Diabetes*. That sounds like a strange disease – you probably have to eat lots of sugar.
While listening to the radio today, I suddenly had the urge to begin an exciting career in law enforcement, medical assisting, court reporting, or get my high school diploma.

Social-Justice *Old Yeller:*

Travis: Ma! Ma! I think Old Yeller's got the homophoby! I seen him
      bitin' everyone in town wearin' pink, and then he gone and peed
      all over Jack and Ennis's flower garden!
Ma *(handing him the rifle):* You know what you gotta do, son. We don't
      tolerate no one disagreein' with us round here.
Travis: Yessum.
Ma: And after that, are you gonna do your math schoolwork?
Travis: Naw, math is racist!
Ma: That's a good boy.
Travis: Wait...how do you know I identify as a boy and not a girl?
Ma: Gagdurn it, I done committed a microagression. Here, hand me
      back that rifle...I know what I gotta do.

Girl 1: I can't wait to go to Africa.
Girl 2: Wow, you're going to Africa?
Girl 1: No, I'm not – that's why I can't wait; if I start waiting I'll never
      stop.

Today a police officer stopped me and said i was speeding so i said no
officer, i wasn't speeding. And he said well you can tell that to the
judge. That seemed like a good idea so i went over to the judge's house
and waited in his bathtub so i could tell him myself. Then when he
came in wearing his bathrobe he looked really surprised to see me and
said "Wow, this must be my birthday gift!"

Sometimes I feel like no one understands me...like when the 911 operator says she doesn't understand why I keep inviting her to go fishing in my hot tub. Well, it seems like a pretty good idea because I've heard you can catch a lot of things in a hot tub!

Man, I'd better learn my ABC's and get a GED or I'll end up on EBT. But first, a little CBD...

My Thanksgiving this year was full of thanks and giving. You see, I was giving the dealer the money, and he said thanks. Then he was giving me the drugs, and I said thanks. It was almost like a transaction!

What's the comparative form of "not bad"?
That premium clam juice is not bad, but this expired clam juice with strawberry pulp is not even worse.

Sometimes I wonder what this praying mantis is praying for. Maybe it's praying to get out of my praying mantis puppet show and back onto the praying mantis construction crew (by day) and exotic dance troupe (by night).

I've read that it's always good to "shop local". That's why I buy from Ramón the street dealer instead of Ramón the Executive Vice-President of Sales for the Southwest Division of the Sinaloa Cartel.

With all this inflation nowadays, shortbread is getting shorter, shortcake is getting shorter still, and even the vegetable shortening is running out before I have enough to grease the entire couch.

Woohoo – it's finally time for my online massage.

To reduce costs, the Hope Diamond will now be replaced by the Hope Cubic Zirconia.

I've decided to found my own Historically Black college. I have it all planned out: all the buildings will be black, all the cars will be black, even the trees will be painted black – it's gonna be Historically black! That way, all the white students will be easy to see.

Next year on Halloween I'm going to give out EZ-Choke™ mini-crayons.

My New Year's resolution this year: Im going to forget how to use apostrophe's.

If you're ever afflicted with a case of diarrhea, just make the best of it – get into a swimming pool and pretend you're a squid.

Wade has it made. In the shade. Wait a minute...Wade, aren't you supposed to be filleting earthworms for this weekend's Surrealist Typhoid Vaccination Party and Bingo?

Well, OK, I suppose I can come in for a minute...

My, this is such a lovely space...and those geraniums!

Hey – Aunt Maxine! Get down from that stripper pole! Did you forget you still have 90 days left on your non-compete? Oh my, her technique isn't what it used to be.

Oh hello, Judge Gibston...sure, I'd like to see an ultrasound[4]...of your 3-year-old...who already looks suspiciously similar to Wade. And I'm glad your wife enjoyed her solo vacation.

Wade: *winks*

Hey - it's my turn on the merry-go-round!

Wade: Actually, it's called a carousel because as you can see it's rotating counter-clockwise.

But wait, there's more! It turns out that Wade has invited me here because he's SUPER excited to offer me an AMAZING opportunity to start my own business and be my own boss! And that sounds great because if I were my own boss I'd say to myself: you know, Phylecia, there are faster ways to get ahead in this company...if you're willing. ☺

Ooh, black mold canapés! Don't mind if I do...

Thanks, chimp butler.

Today is the start of National Volunteer Week. That's great because when I go to the bank they usually tell me I volunteer too much information, like what my blood type is this week, or how many mouth(s) I have. And I thought they needed this information so I can

---

[4] Never offer to show me the ultrasound.

rent their ponies but the teller said sorry, the ponies are only for High Net Worth clients. So I leaned in and whispered real quiet-like, so what else do you do for these clients? And he leaned in and said meet me in the parking lot after we close, come alone and no police. So I said OK no police but how about Boy Scouts? I have a few of those stashed in an abandoned refrigerator at my place. And he said there you go again with your too much information. Weird because I didn't even tell him the model number of the refrigerator, which is KTP-0191A and features a spacious variable-humidity produce bin. And no Brayden you can't have another Girl Scout cookie, they might make you confused about your gender and plus have you seen how expensive they're getting lately? I know but you'll learn this someday and why don't you grow up and get a job.

So anyway, happy National Volunteer Week!

You learn something new every day. Today I learned that scrap metal dealers don't accept stop signs, shopping carts, traffic lights, or hip implants.

I've got a rumbly in my tumbly. A quick search of the medical literature suggests that it's a perforated hemorrhagic ulcer of the pylorus. ☺

I suspect I may have contracted lemonAIDS. It's actually a very refreshing disease, plus I wasn't really using that immune system anyway. And I can always borrow someone else's. *(cough)* this afternoon i was riding my Big Wheels in the hotel hallway and this ball rolled right in front of me and luckily i'd installed anti-lock brakes so I was able to stop in time. and then these two little girls appeared and invited me to play with them forever, and ever, and ever. so i thought well ok they're pretty hot, even though they called me Danny for some reason lol. so we went into room 237 because the door was open and one thing led to another! so now am i supposed to get both their phone numbers?

While I was doing some spring cleaning, I needed a small box to store some items. So I wrote "sm. box" on my shopping list. Later, while at the store, I looked at the list and thought, hmm, I didn't know I needed an S&M box, but I guess so, since it's on the list. Unfortunately, they were out of stock...but I had an idea. So when I arrived back home I turned on the Naughty Hallmark Channel and watched a few rounds of *S&M Boxing Challenge XII – Live from Westchester Senior Living Community.* As you might imagine, this facility is suitably advertised for "active seniors". Oops, they just threw the penalty flag again...Grandma, I told you that was an illegal move! Looks like I'm going to have to write her a Negative Performance Review.

My 25-year-old buddy Phil was having a drink at a bar when he was stealthily approached by a cougar! Luckily he was carrying Cougar-Off™ repellent spray. It works by making you look 20 years older. Cougars soon lose interest and wander off, foraging in the nearest refuse bin for discarded food.

My manager cheerfully sent our team a message advising us to have a productive shift. So I did, since I always follow directions to the letter. But in this case her "F" key wasn't working, so now I'm thoroughly cleaning my office chair.

Oh no – I've been sucked into the Pornado! It's an Exciting Whirlwind of Adult Entertainment™.
It seems the Lifetime Network is becoming rather desperate for viewers.

I thought I'd misplaced my mustache, but it was right under my nose the whole time. I really should tell the lice to stop moving it around so I never forget where it is.

Culinary arts professor: ...and artful presentation is important because
        we eat with the eyes first.
Cannibal student: Um, professor...so do I eat the eyes with the eyes
        first?

Customer: Excuse me, I'm looking for a chemical to clean my
        swimming pool.
Hardware clerk: Well, this here's hydrochloric acid; it's your basic acid,
        so you can ...
Chemistry professor *(climbing through the shelf, paint cans clattering)*: Now,
        wait just a minute...

1: Hey, what are you doing tonight?

2: Well, I was planning to expect the unexpected, but it hasn't exactly worked out as I'd anticipated.

1: Well, did you use that EXPEKTAVATOR(tm) I got you?

2: Yeah, but it didn't meet my expectations.

1: So it was working perfectly, then.

2: Yep - I love being disappointed! There are so many ways for something to go wrong, you never know what's going to leave you deflated next! Oh, and can you loosen my neck restraint a little? It's kinda hard to breathe amidst the excitement of all these letdowns.

1: Sure, here you go.

2: Hey, you tightened it!

1: Surprise! Disappointed?

2. You bet! :)

You may have noticed that many men's names can be turned into women's names just by changing the ending to -ie.
For example: Bobby, Bill, and Steve become Bobbie, Billie, and Stevie. Now, I'd like to introduce my lady friends Stanlie, Larrie, and Grandpappie.

You've probably heard about the little trick of putting a marshmallow in the bottom of an ice cream cone to prevent dripping. But for younger children, I've found that a small marble works much better.

I want to start carrying a clicking device around and click it every time I blink my eyes while having a conversation.

Uh-oh, Mrs. Butterworth is talkin' dirty.

The police stopped me for exceeding the speed limit in the Friend Zone. Apparently I was getting nowhere with that chick WAAAY too fast.

No, Officer, I don't have a...what did you call it? 'Driver's License'. That's a funny word!

Her: *(sigh)* I just don't feel like adulting today...

Me: Well, you could try calving, which involves producing whale offspring. Or if you prefer, you could split off a chunk of glacier to form an iceberg. This may be a difficult procedure! Is no recommend.

Doctor: Patient is presenting with intermittent neuralgia affecting the lower transverse colon, appears to be idiopathic...

Patient: Now wait a minute, doctor – I know I'm telepathic; that's how I knew your secretary was eight months pregnant (not my fault this time btw), but you don't have to call me a idiot. And can I get another lollipop? The first one tasted like crap and didn't even have a stick.

Doctor: You mean another suppository?

Patient: ...don't you have some docting to do, Dr. Anus?

Doctor: That's *Anaïs!*

Me (on the phone): ...yeah, my date's gonna be over in like 3 minutes but hey I gotta go make a donation to charity.

Charitee (in bed next to me): Actually, it's not really a donation, but more of a "fee rendered for an entertainment service" – at least that's what the IRS thinks, anyway.

Me: OK, then could I get a receipt?

Charitee: Sure, I guess...hey Ra'seet, you almost done in the shower?

Ra'seet (sticking her head out of the shower): Whoa, I've never done a three-way before!

Charitee: Actually, it's more of a "value-added service enhancement" –
at least that's what corporate billing says.

Dang...I seem to have misplaced the keys to my FunCuffs™. And my
bus stop is coming up soon.
No, Jazzlyn, you can't have another dog biscuit. How about a nice cat
biscuit?

I saw a product called a Kink-Free Hose. But that doesn't sound very
exciting – I like my hose kinky.

If you refer to your spouse as your ex-fiancée, technically you're not
wrong.[5]

I was browsing some travel accessories and came across something
called a Hanging Toiletry Kit. This must be for when you're on vacation
in Upper Crackistan and get lonely or run out of drugs or the local
"unofficial" police department tries to shake you down for your last
bottle of imitation jackfruit & clam brandy so you decide to hang
yourself in the toilet. These celebrities who are content to simply use a
belt or bedsheet really should be using the right tool for the job. It's not
like they can't afford it – I think we're witnessing the decline of culture
here.

---

[5] Unless he's male, in which case the rules of French grammar say that
technically you *are* wrong.

My girlfriend called me today and said there's something she has to tell me, and I should probably get tested. Oh boy, I wonder what I win if I pass the test. I like surprises!
You might not like this one so much, she says.

1: Hey, look, that sign says Japanese.
2: No, it says Jalapeños.
1: *(giggling)* Heehee, hall of *what?*
2: Oh, grow up, Reverend!

As the saying goes, there's no use crying over spilled milk.
Spilled Louis XIII Cognac, on the other hand...

The problem with computers is that they do what you tell them to, rather than what you want them to.

As we learned today in Hip-Hop Nuclear Geophysics class, fissures be fission.

Why are there so many people in the Middle East named Al?

I keep getting CD's in the mail from this company called America Online. The packaging says that I can use this service to talk to other

people's computers over the phone line. But why would I do that? If I
want to talk to someone's computer I'll just sneak into their bedroom at
night and talk to it myself. That way I can look the machine in the eye
and tell whether it's lying about those subprime mortgage refinancing
offers, my long-overdue foreign lottery winnings, and che@p V1@gra,
which supposedly makes me popular with the ladies.[6] And if it won't
talk, I have ways of making it talk. Like this powerful magnet here,
which doesn't exactly get along well with hard drives. Or this cup of
soda with the lid that isn't quite fitted tightly...and my hands are feeling
a little shaky at the moment. You see, people don't seem to recognize
the many hidden dangers (and me) lurking in their bedrooms.
And when I'm finished dealing with that computer, it's on to the
underwear drawer. I like trying on the pink ones because they look
somewhat like mine, except they aren't as lacy and soiled. Soilent Pink, I
call them. But look, a telephone...I can use it to call someone's
computer. I hope it answers in a sultry voice and asks what I'm wearing
because I've just slipped on the handcuffs I discovered in the sock
drawer, apparently mis-filed. I'll have to tell my Book Club all about this
experience because it would make great alternative children's literature
for Story Time with Escaped Convicts. And maybe the convicts can
show me how to get out of these handcuffs.

The autocorrect feature on my phone is becoming rather bothersome.
When I typed "private property", it was randomly changed to "Pirate
Pornparty", which is quite odd since I've never even seen that movie 51
times using my neighbor's stolen password. Never ever.

---

[6] It doesn't say which ladies, so that doesn't really do me any good.

Last night, after a round of drinks, I brought my date to my place and showed her around with the typical introductory tour. When we came to my bedroom, I winked and said, "This is where the magic happens, you know...."

"Oh, really?" she replied with a sly curl of her lips, "Well then, are you gonna impress me?"

So I carried off a rousing performance of my magic show, titled "Maybe You Shouldn't Have Left Your Drink Unattended"[7].

She commented astutely on the felicitous viewing angles and my adroit legerdemain techniques. I remarked that she had just used two contiguous French loanwords. Not to be outdone, she countered by observing that the rabbit I'd pulled out of the hat appeared to be in an advanced state of decomposition.

"*Mais oui,*" I agreed, "judging by the density of blowflies (*Calliphora vicina*) I'd estimate the time of death to be sometime after the series finale of *Dawson's Creek* but prior to yesterday."

My guest suggested that since we were given to using French *vocabulaire*, maybe we should introduce a *cliché*. So we proceeded to *grimper aux rideaux*, 'twixt wind and water, until *la petit mort*, whereupon I sent her home in *le taxi*.

Remember, Mom said, boys are only interested in one thing. I'm pretty sure she meant my Anatomy homework. See, Freddie's already got his camera out...he's always trying to get a look at my Anatomy.

---

[7] Generously sponsored by GHB Anæsthesia Supply!

Here's an interesting fact: the average person spends a total of 38 days of their life brushing their teeth. Now, I know how important good dental hygiene is, so it looks like I'm going to be a bit unavailable until around October 19.

(*sigh*) You know, some days all I feel like doing is swim, and eat, and make little sharks...that's all!

Today I returned to my car after performing some bizarre activity which suitably serves as a joke setup[8] and found that someone had dented the door. Who would do such a thing, I thought, when I realized my mistake.
Pro tip: never park too close to a dentist. They are extremely skilled at denting and then escaping without detection. And they're immune to x-rays! Just don't x-ray the trunk, or I might have to "explain" a few things.

When people ask me, "Why haven't you gotten married yet? Haven't you found the right person?" My reaction is, "Why haven't you stabbed yourself in the eye yet? Haven't you found the right pencil?"

Woohoo, I can't wait for next week – it's time for Tapeworm Safari! Dust off your miniature canoe and don't make any sudden movements.

---

[8] Metahumor!

Today at my dentist appointment I was chatting with a really attractive hygienist; as we continued flirting I knew things were going to heat up when she put away the x-ray machine and brought out the XXX-ray machine.

Oh boy, I sure hope this is covered by my insurance! I know how complicated insurance can be; it turns out that they cover home visits by a nurse, but not by a "NUR$E".

umm so i just heard mom talking to her friend about where babies come from! but now i'm kinda confused because i don't have a boss and i don't know where the supply closet is when his assistant is hanging around and she won't leave and what's a jealousy complex? mom said she hopes I don't find out but i think i just found out! ☺ now i'm going to impress her with my knowledge at the next family gathering.

While visiting New York City, I elected to take a guided tour organized by my hotel. The concierge informed me that I should come to the lobby the following morning to meet my tour guides, Vic and Moe. Wow, I thought, those are some authentically New York-sounding names; these two are sure to have plenty of insider knowledge about the city! The next morning I went down to the lobby, and besides a number of guests milling around, I wasn't sure where my guides were to be found. Near the door I spotted a small crowd gathered around two gentlemen, one Indian, the other Middle Eastern,. So I went over and asked them where the tour group was meeting with Vic and Moe. I was informed that these were my guides, Vikram and Mohammed.

If you donate a large sum of money to a community college, would they award you an honorary Associate's?

If I have no tolerance for lactose intolerance, does that mean I'm tolerant or intolerant?

I heard a song urging me to party like it's 1999. You know what that means – get out the America Online CD's that come in the mail every week, dial up the Bulletin Board service, and invite my friends over for Zima and Bartles & Jaymes wine coolers. And while they're here we can plan our trip to see the World Trade Center, but that probably won't be for a few years since my career at Enron is just taking off. I pity whoever isn't buying that hot stock since they don't have the foresight that I do. Ooh, my friend is paging me...time to go see the new Phantom Menace movie, and I just know it's gonna be awesome! And if a certain Jar Jar Binks delivers the performance I think he will, I'm totally voting for him for Character of the Year.[9]
So anyway, party on!

I like to eavesdrop on my parents and last night I heard them saying they wanted to spice things up in the bedroom for a change. I thought to myself, I know, I'll help! And I know where they keep the spice rack in the kitchen so I went and sprinkled oregano in their bed, just like the rose petals from that movie I wasn't allowed to see but my dad is always looking at the poster in the bathroom. Then today my mom said she

---

[9] Sorry, Rob Schneider.

was really itchy and she asked my dad hey are you sure that goat didn't have fleas? And he said yeah the guy at the rental place guaranteed she was clean. And my mom said, "SHE???"

Next time I think they should build a large wooden badger.

Recent genealogical research has revealed that the fabled Humpty Dumpty was actually known in his time as Humptius Dumptikos IV, embattled monarch of an obscure, short-lived Proto-Balto-Slavic nation-state. As we know, he ultimately met his untimely demise at the cruel hands of the force of gravity. Alas, his loyal staff was unable to reassemble him because he had chosen them based on diversity rather than their abilities. And thus he perished.

Now, what's this I hear about history repeating itself?

Today I was looking for a pair of scissors because I had to sciss something. Sciss is a funny, foreign-looking word. Now, I don't speak Flemish, but if I did I'd wonder where i could find a country called Flem, so I could go and speak to those fine people in their own language, which probably involves a significant number of guttural phonemes. The last time I attempted this kind of cross-cultural exchange, I tried speaking Curdish to the poutine-eating people of Canadia, who know the way of curds like no other race of people on Earth. Thinking that their tribe would be open to trading with the white man, I went to their trading post and presented 1.2 kg of curds and asked how much do you whey? The chieftain, apparently displeased that I wasn't speaking his native Quebbeckian language, must not have liked this question because he called upon his tribe's finely honed diplomacy skills and punched me in the mouth and mentioned something about hockey.
O Canadia, have you no *dentistes?*

The first step of knowledge is knowing what it is that you don't know. And once you know what you don't know, just go ahead and know it! Unfortunately, if there's one thing I know, it's that I'm not very good at knowing things.
You there! Could you know something for me?
Hurry up, know faster!

Lifeguard: No running!
My bowels: Ha! We'll show him!
          ...right, gas-station sushi?

(sigh) I really should get better at wearing shoes. Sometimes I put them on the wrong hands, and other times I don't pour in enough kerosene for proper ignition (at least without a #6 glow plug). But I'm studying hard, and the psychiatric nurse says that's what counts. And the purple elephant over there agrees...sure, Mr. Blopper, I'd love to start a fire. The chemical storage closet? You read my mind. ☺

Colonel: Gentlemen, in our staff meeting today I was informed that a few of our men were partying a little too much and had to be taken by MP's to something called the Drunk Tank. Now I don't know anything about that but it sounds like it's like a regular tank only it does funny things because it's drunk. Like instead of rolling over enemy vehicles it just sits there and spins its turret around until the people inside get dizzy and they'd have to come out and kiss whoever it's pointing to. And then it could discharge its sewage reservoir all over them, just like a real drunkard! Sweet – I'm totally including this in my next procurement order.

Lt. al-Aqabwa: Yes, yes, Colonel, and here is pretend tea kettle you ask for.

Colonel.: It's pronounced "colonial". Just put it over there with my Barbies, I mean my Junior Auxiliary Regiment. But don't step on any mines – it's almost tea time and they're doing yoga. By the way, I like that padded vest you're wearing. Did you wire it yourself?

Lt. al-Aqabwa: *(raising his arms)* Allahu Akb—

Colonel: Dismissed.

Lt. al-Aqabwa: Aww, was just getting to good part.

While browsing through the world atlas, I learned that there is a fellow named Chad who lives in central Africa – and apparently has an entire country named after him! Or, perhaps he's just extremely large (unlike his diminutive neighbor, a certain Mr. Burkina Faso). If I were this gentleman's homie I would thusly inquire: Yo, where all the white women at? Thereupon he would proffer a prodigious prospectus of pretties for my perusal. Presently, without prattle, I would carefully consider, compare and contemplate, and set forth my selection: how about this one, named Ngekegwe M'dokmubwa, she be lookin' fine. And with a droll chortle comes his bemused retort: my good man, I don't think this is the accoutrement you had in mind. Perhaps you would like to avail yourself of one of our Beckys? They are ex-MLM and very Coachable. Yes, that will do nicely, I reply. Excellent choice, sir, up in here. Please deliver her to the carriage-house, where I shall arrive on the morrow in my hooptie.

As you can see, my study of geography has heretofore proven advantageous. Now, I can only imagine what treasures are to be found in the exotic locales of Turkey, Whales, and Grease...

It turns out that there's an organization called the Juvenile Diabetes Research Foundation. But why are they making juveniles do the research? Maybe the adults tried to find a cure but failed so they said to themselves, well, maybe we should leave it to the kids because you know sometimes kids are better at figuring things out than adults, like phones, electronics, and immunoglobulin receptors. While they're doing that, let's go play Super Mario Bros. and get loaded.

Great news: I've gotten a promotion and a big raise at work! So now I think it's long past time to upgrade my iron lung to a diamond-encrusted platinum lung (with spinning rims, of course). Now the other gunshot victims in the neighborhood will have nothing on me! (Except for those embarrassing photos, of course.)
Pile on in, ladies; there's plenty of oxygen for everyone. But no cameras this time.

    While attending a professional conference, I met quite a few interesting people working for my company. Introducing myself to an attendee hailing from one of our out-of-state office locations, I asked him his name. He extended his hand and replied, "Garrett Lewis."
    Ahh, a name I recognized – a colleague from my home office! There's no better way to make connections than name-dropping. Now, his request was admittedly puzzling, but I did as he asked, sensing a possible accolade (dare I say promotion?) in the air. After all, I had no idea what his motivation might be, or the nature of his corporate connections. And today's business climate surely can be cut-throat!
    When I'd finished garroting Louis, I turned again to this mysterious gentleman and once again asked his name.

Dinner Guest: My goodness, Georgie! This pudding is wonderful...and the pie, what a fabulously tender crust!
Georgie: Why, thank you...I had just enough time after work to get these into the oven. I know they look store-bought, but I actually kissed the girls myself and made them cry.
Guest: Wait...what???

(from down the hallway): Daddy!!

Georgie: Girls, I told you I'm not your real Daddy. Now go finish your telemarketing.

(Knock at the door)

Police Officer: Mr. Porgie? We'd like to have a word with you....

Georgie: Sorry, gotta run!

(Cut to Announcer): Folks, don't let this happen to you. If you're going to visit random prison inmates and smuggle them out with the laundry, be sure to put them in a *dirty* laundry bin, or the guards will ask you why you're wheeling out the clean laundry, and you'll have to make up a story such as the hotel next door ran out of linens because the huge Death Metal Bluegrass festival is in town and the headliner, Virgin Tractor Decapitation, brought way too many assistants and their washing machine is broken because one of them used it to dry her cat, but it wasn't specifically stated in the instructions that you couldn't do that, so she successfully sued the manufacturer and was awarded 2.4 million rupees since she accidentally went to a court in India because that's where her cab driver was from and it was late in the day so he absentmindedly just drove home forgetting that he had a passenger.

(Announcer's phone rings): Hello? .... No, I don't want to buy into a time share. And take me off of your telemarketing list, young lady. ...What am I *wearing?*

7:00 Breakfast

8:00 Break out

9:00 Break in

10:00 Break down

11:00 Break news

12:00 Break up

1:00 Break time

2:00 Breakdance

3:00 Breakthrough

5:00 Breakdown

When I finally decided to propose to my girlfriend, I thought I'd surprise her by doing it at one of her improv comedy group rehearsals. I was quite happy when she said "Yes, and...."

Five minutes later, we had all the details worked out: we'd rent out the extra bedroom in our pretend RV on the nights Scientology Cookie Monster[10] isn't subletting it to the Cocaine Figure-Skating Jihad or hosting paid intimate nights with Covid-Squid™ (but don't call it a side hustle because technically he's just accepting tips [which he calls a "suggested donation"]). And we also learned that it's hard to pantomime nested parentheses.

Meanwhile, the rest of the group performers started taking bets about how long we'd last before we split up. They decided it would be until one of the audience members stepped in and took my place. And wouldn't you know, suddenly one of the audience members jumped in and said, "Stop! Now you're Superman!"

Nice try, lil' Mikey, but I'm not into superhero role play with boys your age.

Woman (*on phone*): "I can't wait...we're going to spend the evening together. You know, it was love at first sight. We've been together for 5 years now....Of course she's romantic; I like feeling her beside me while I sleep, I like the way she cuddles with me, the way she smells....Well, she's a little younger; she'll be 5 this month....Yeah, I know *you* understand....Hold on, I've gotta go, Vince just brought her home from her vet appointment. I have to change her water dish. Then she's going to give me an erotic girl-on-girl massage while Vince films it. Later!

---

[10] le Monstre des Biscuits

Announcer: Don't miss tonight's steamy new episode of *Dog Mom*, now
on Adults Only Video.
Director: Cut! OK, nice job, folks…let's get this set rearranged for the
next shot. Amanda, can you clean up all this dog hair? It's getting
all over the camera lens.
Junior High Principal: Wow, we're so glad you could come to our
Women's Career Day – it really helps us educate our students
about their career options in the entertainment industry. *(Picks
up microphone)*: And remember, girls, there will be "auditions" in
my office after school today. Come alone.

My politically correct HOA is really concerned about "inclusion",
so they required me to take down my Christmas lights and replace them
with Holiday lights. But they didn't say which holiday, so I chose
National Put a Dead Fish in Everyone's Mailbox Day (even though it's
not *officially* recognized, but hey, since we're being inclusive).

The next day the neighborhood cat gang came around and said
hey boss, we hear you have something we want, and it might be spelled
F-I-S-H but you didn't hear that from us. Now, I'm not gonna pussyfoot
around, see? If you don't cooperate, me and the boys here'll have to
make you disappear purrmanently, fur reals. And I said wow, Mr.
Noodles, those are some intimidating brass knuckles – did you get them
from the Rabbit of Caerbannog? And he said don't worry about that
but if you see him tell him I don't have his $200. And then he pulled
out a picture of my kids and said it would be a real shame if something
were to happen to the brakes on their school bus. And I said wow, Mr.
Noodles, you seem a little upset. Would it help to talk about it? And he
sighed well, this gender transition is really taking a toll on my peer

credibility, so my therapist says apparently I'm seeking external validation of my insecurities, even from individuals who don't affirm my values, which isn't self-actualizing. Especially with a name like Mr. Noodles, when all my homies here have names like Clawde, Lawnmeower, and Thørvald G. Flüfftensen, Esq. Not only that, I just found out my former mate is FIV-pawsitive. It turns out he's been wandering around the alleyways at dusk, so I suspect he's, you know...crepuscular. He's probably in a stupor somewhere right now, strung out on the 'nip.[11]

Just then, out of nowhere, the mail truck rolled by, and it would be a real shame if Mr. Noodles didn't get out of the way quite in time because while he was talking I discreetly stood on his tail. Oooh, that's gotta hurt. And the brass knuckles go flying and oops, sorry Mr. Vandenberg, no you can just keep those; they're actually good for scraping fish out of a mailbox.

And this is why a man shall leave his Homeowners' Association and cling to his wife's Botox therapist, and the two become friends with benefits, until it comes out that each of their respective spouses are also secretly having an affair, when in a stroke of sitcom-inspired coincidence they all meet awkwardly at the punch bowl at the community ~~Christmas~~ Holiday party.

Woman 1: Looking back over the years, I think the best feeling I've ever
        had was when my grandchildren were born.
Woman 2: Wow, I can't imagine how that must have felt. So how did
        that work, did you deliver their mother first and she's like
        come on kids I can't wait around all day, Mommy has things

---

[11] Now with fentanyl!

to do and that wine isn't gonna drink itself! Or did the kids come first because they didn't want to wait they're turn[12] and she's like hey wait for me, stay where I can see you and don't cross the street by yourselves!

Today I got a bill in the mail for a product or service I never received. It's for $0.00 (plus interest!) and now they're trying to collect but I don't have that kind of money! So they threatened to come and take my house. But I told them I don't have a house, so they offered to just give me one and then come and repossess it and I'd be out on the street. So I said OK that's very nice of you and actually it sounds like a pretty good idea since it's a nice day today and I could use a walk so I'll just wait here by the front door that I don't have and meanwhile maybe I can finally straighten this crooked doorjamb so it doesn't stick so much when the dog catcher shows up and hands me a package but he's mistaken because it says "dog catheter", and do I look like a Vietnam veterinarian? Or when the imaginary pizza deliveryman shows up and I answer the door in my bathrobe and it "accidentally" falls off. Yep, better fix that door, now gotta go find a drill to hammer in those loose screws.

And hello, intoxicated walrus podiatrist, sure you can drive my imaginary car but this time make sure you roll the windows up and remember to put 89 octane in it, but the more important question is how did you get the number to my car-phone?

---

[12] She thinks "they're" is a possessive since it contains an apostrophe. Stupid young people dont' know anything and.

Today I received a notice in the mail informing me that if I fell down a flight of parquet-covered stairs in southern North County in northern South Dakota between 1986 and 1987, I could be entitled to monetary compensation!

But upon exhaustive research (including a number of conversations with lovely telephone operator Jolene, who after several attempts stubbornly refuses to tell me what she's wearing and appears increasingly rattled with each subsequent call, especially after I successfully guess her license plate number – what are the odds?[13]), it appears that this offer does not apply in certain narrowly defined circumstances. For example, suppose (hypothetically) that an admittedly disreputable, chronically underemployed cat were to convince me that flinging myself down the aforementioned stairs would serve as enough civil disobedience to persuade the TV networks to bring my beloved Street Hawk back on the air, which they've subsequently refused to do, despite much camping out on the execs' front lawns and teaching their dogs to play reverse fetch. (go hide the insulin, good boy! here is some chocolate)

Fortunately, I do have the address of the law firm and a full box of matches. So perhaps constructing a miniature matchstick replica of Hegyhátszentmárton Castle ca. 1589 will be enough to persuade them

---

[13] In a seven-digit permutation of letters and numbers, this probability is equal to:

$$_nP_r = \frac{36!}{(36-7)!}$$

$$= 1 : 42{,}072{,}307{,}200$$

But then you have to subtract 1 from the denominator since her plate can't be the same as mine, which is STRTHWK.

to award me All the Money I Deserve™. But if not, there are other ways...isn't that right, treacherously deceptive (but peculiarly convincing) cat?

Oooh, but it's hard for kitty to talk since he's preserved in a jar of formaldehyde, which is more properly called methanal, except that that word ends with "-anal" so everyone on the school bus (who looks at me rather oddly since I'm 37) tends to giggle and purposefully mispronounce it, at least until the formaldehyde (methanal) kicks in and their eyes glaze over. You know, maybe it's time to buy stock in a chemical supply company, if this is going to become a regular thing.

A friend of mine said that last weekend she went out for brunch, which is a combination of breakfast and lunch. But I'm going to do even better than that with clunch, a combination of cocaine and lunch.

Whatever you do, don't look up the Czech translation for "bubble blower".

I'm proud of how well I've stuck to my new low-carb diet; there's been a chocolate cake sitting in my kitchen all week and I haven't even touched it.

Well, I have touched it, but not...you know..."down there". This diet doesn't go *that* low on carbs.

This weekend at church my pastor said we should Pray the Gay Away. So I tried that for a while but it didn't work. So then I thought maybe I could Spray the Gay Away. And it worked! He must have been allergic to the UV dye in this pepper spray because he took off in a hurry!

With all this talk of renewable energy and wind farms, I wonder whose job it is to clean up all the wind manure? Since it's so windy it probably blows all over the place so you have to run after it with a butterfly net and when you catch it you deposit it into the special scoring receptacle and the first team to score 10 points wins! And now put your hands together for our mascot Stoolie the pigeon, who will do a flyover! But watch out, he's got a massive case of diarrhea because you all have been tossing him scraps of white bread instead of whole grains. So we sure hope you picked up your stain-resistant Dungbrella at rhe concession stand, because they're all sold out.
And here he comes!

Today at work someone suddenly began stumbling around and gasping about having a medical emergency but i thought he said a medical 'imagine-cy', so i didn't do anything because that means he was just pretending.[14] And oops, down he goes. So then while i was trying to get my toast to land butter-side-up the ambulance people came and picked him up off the floor and draped a white sheet over him so i thought oh wow, now he's pretending to be a scary ghost who hires people to push him around on a cart so people think the place is haunted. Working at a hospital is fun!

---

[14] and i don't understand Australian accents anyway.

Last night I was in the mood to mate. So I decided to go see my friend Nate, who also likes to mate. When I arrived at his place I tiptoed into his bedroom, being careful not to trip on any of the harnesses or restraints lying around. (He is very adventurous!) I poked him a bit but he didn't respond, so it seemed as though he didn't want to mate. I just figured he was being very shy or asleep, so I took out a #4 slotted screwdriver and tried to make some slight adjustments to correct this malfunction. But that didn't work and he still didn't want to mate. Suddenly, Farmer Brown came running into the barn and shouted hey you freak what are you doing here again, I told you to stay away from the sheep!

And that wasn't very nice.

Fortunately, it turns out that someone[15] had sharpened the screwdriver into a fine 0.006" bevel.

Oh my, now I've made quite a mess. But not to worry – luckily I studied Crime Scene Evidence Disposal at the Mop-Tech Janitorial Academy (a division of the Consolidated University of Custodial Arts), so I know exactly how to make this go away. But in any case, it looks like Nate is going to need a new boyfriend. And I happen to know just the guy! ☺

Right, Nate?

Baaaa, said Nate.

Last night I dreamed I went to a brothel but there were long lines. So tomorrow night I'm going somewhere else.

---

[15] I'm not telling!

Almost finished with your chemistry homework, mein Schatz?
Almost! I just have to figure out one final solution, but I'm pretty sure the answer is "chlorine".

This morning when I awoke, feeling rather groggy, I reached for my cool, refreshing eye drops. Moist-tastic!™ But instead, I inadvertently picked up my ear wax removal drops, which were beside them on the shelf. So now it seems I've removed all of my eye wax. You know what that means: the eye-bees (*Apis oculomellifera*)[16] will have to start getting their honey from the local "distributor" like everyone else up in the hood instead of cooking it themselves. But they'd better finish that batch in a hurry because the eye-bears (*Ursus ophthalmicus*) are arriving soon and don't like being strung out without their fix of honey. And you wouldn't like them when they're angry: it's even worse than when Winnie-the-Pooh got mad when Tigger[17] cheated on him with Christopher Robin's drag hairstylist and the whole forest found out about it so he burned down the salon in a jealous rage, but the prosecutor said it was OK because Winnie was a first-time offender and we don't want to send too many of THOSE people to jail, so let's go after the lighter fluid manufacturer instead and claim their advertising was irresponsible. Just don't get *that* stuff mixed up with your eye drops, or you'll end up hosting an eye-B-Q.[18]

---

[16] NB: Just don't call them I.B.'s. It may sound the same to humans, but the bees' sensitive ears* can tell the difference. If you do this they will become agitated and you'll have to bring out the smoke pot.**

[17] The editors regret the use of this archaic term, which was in common use at the time this text was written. We now use the more acceptable term Tigerian-American.

[18] NB: But don't use the term I.B.Q. (see above). Although in this case, using a smoke pot would enhance the depth of flavor of the ocular tissue, with the vitreous humor acting as a self-basting mechanism. The editors recommend using mesquite or hickory for best results.

---

* Correct, bees don't have ears, but come on, this is a f****g comedy book.

It can be rather awkward to run into your boss outside of work. Earlier this week I was driving around downtown and happened to see mine. My first thought was, wow, she usually doesn't wear a skirt *that* short at the office, nor a leopard-print bra (it's usually zebra). Secondly, I noticed that she was surreptitiously asking random passersby hey honey, are u lookin for a date? So I thought OK, why not, I guess a date sounds like fun. So we arranged our little "date," though sometimes she calls it a "party" or a "soirée," which are code words indicating how much she plans to charge based on her sliding scale, which appears to be a first in the industry. Afterwards I advised her that after a thoroughly stimulating evaluation, her Work Product Rating (WPR2) came in at about 80% of quarterly cost-center expectations, so I regret to inform you that we're sorry but we cannot justify allotting you a bonus this quarter, although we look forward to your continued efforts to positively reflect our corporate values.

Just then my coworker hiding in the trunk whispered, *"Do you think she's a diversity hire too?"* Annoyed, I replied, "Shut up, Mbakembwe,[19] that's racist."

Child: Mom! The babysitter tried to harvest my organs AGAIN!
Mother: So...remember what we talked about – did she have a permit?
Child: Umm...yeah but only a Class 2 permit but she was trying to get
      Class 3 organs.

** Hehe, I said "smoke pot". *(cough)*

[19] Señor Mbakembwe Donatellio von Aixesse III. Actually, his real name is Yechmiel Goldschlapp, but due to a head injury he thinks he's Nigerian, and he would have had me fooled except for the Brooklyn accent and the white pigmentation, which he insists is the result of a government conspiracy.

Mother: *(sigh)* We've been over this...what do you do in that case?

Child: Umm...grant an easement?

Mother: No – it's a *variance!* There's a difference! You'll need to know this when you go to China to work in the shoe factory. Believe me, they're experts at this.

Child: Aww, do I have to?

Mother: Well, how else are we going to afford your brother's gender transition?

Child: Aww, rats!

Mother: Yes, there will be plenty of rats. Now, I have to give your brother his bottle, I mean her bottle, so go put on your mailman costume – it's almost time for you to dance.

At the post office:

Postal worker 1: Hey AL, do you want to ZIP out to the bar and get some WY NE?

Postal worker 2: HI, MO. Actually, my MD said I should cut down IN the future, so ID avoid it.

1: OH, OK. WY?

2: Well, my PA was an alcoholic. Plus it makes me feel IL and I get severe diarrhea - it's like MT St. Helens!

1: AK! tMI! Maybe another time; it's not really a Priority. So are your folks still living in NH?

2: Yes, they AR.

1: Didn't your dad work for ND Smith & CO? OR was that someone else?

2: Yeah, but then he went back to school and got an MA at NC State.

1: Cool, my manager MS. Barron went there too. That school is DE
   best!
2: So...what's going ON with Fred? You know, the guy we had PE class
   with back in the day?
1: Well, I heard a rumor that he's GA.
2: Hehe, do you think he's the sender or the recipient?
1: Right, dude, maybe we should overnight him some KY. I just hope
   he doesn't try to KS me in the sorting room.
Fred: Who, ME?
1: Uh-oh...he looks PO'd.

At a restaurant:
Host: Good day, sir, can I help you?
Customer: Hello, can I talk to your Vietnamese cousin?
Host: Sorry, sir, I don't understand.
Customer: Your sign outside says "Vietnamese Cousin", right?
Host: It says "Vietnamese *Cuisine*".
Customer: Quã-sinh? That's a funny name, but it sure sounds
         Vietnamese. So like if I offer her 5 dollar, she'll—
Host: Sir, this isn't that kind of place.
Customer: Oh boy, where can I find that kind of place? ☺
Host: Well, in this neighborhood, there is an establishment about a
         block north of here, at the corner of Crystal St, and Meths Ave.,
         on the right.
Customer: Umm...you mean the one called "The Happy Message"?
Host: It actually says "Thai Happy Massage".
Customer: Tie? Oh goody, my old Scout Master showed me how to tie
         all kinds of knots. He said they were useful for...certain things that

I shouldn't tell my parents about, but don't worry, it's perfectly natural.

Host: Umm...well, I'm sure they would be happy to accommodate your...needs. Now, would you like to order something?

Customer: *(glancing at the menu)* Hmm...which do you recommend, Mỹ Dung or Phāic Rất Dong?

Host: Well, I usually order both and then dunk the Dong in the Dung.

Customer: Wow, do they let you do that at The Happy Message too?

Host: Well, yes, but it's not on the menu and it costs a little extra.

Customer: That's OK; I usually leave without paying anyway.

Host: Excellent choice, sir.

Customer: I'll take both of those to go.

Host: I'm afraid Tu Ngô no longer works here, as she left to accept a position at Punishment Palace Chinese Buffet. You've probably heard their slogan: *"If you don't leave crying, was no spicy enough!"*

Customer: No MSG?

Host: No MSG.

Girl 1: Mom says I'm blossoming into a beautiful Flower! And she says pretty soon the boys will come and try to Pollinate me.

Girl 2: Umm, I don't know what that means. . .

Girl 1: I don't either, but she says the important thing is, don't give it away for free!

"Hey man, it's been a long time! Still dealing with that UTI?"[1]

"I sure am! Right now I'm helping them convert their LSD[2] into PCP."[3]

"Sounds good, but you'd better be careful; if you don't follow all the "special" rules, you might get a call from the FBI[4] inquiring why you haven't paid your fees to the IRS.[5] And of course, they could even get RICO[6] after you."

"Don't I know it. Last time I was graced with a surprise visit from him, he gave me COVID,[7] and I was filling out forms for a week! I had to report where I got my MBA[8] and the name of my CPA[9] so they could send some incriminating photos back to their colleagues in DC[10] via UPS.[11] And the next day his goons even showed up at my place to take me for a little ride in their BMW[12] for a little R&R.[13] What a bunch of fascists! I mean, what is this, the TSA?"[14]
"That's rough, man…but at least they didn't make you show them your PP[15] like they did with me. That was embarrassing, especially in front of all the VIP's![16] But anyway, what are you doing this weekend?"

---

1. Unaccredited Training Institute
2. Legal-ish Studies Department
3. Pharmaceutical Counterfeiting Practice
4. Fake Building Inspector
5. Illicit Revenue Squad
6. Martinelli, Esq.
7. Criminal Organization Verification/Intake Documents
8. Mexican Blow Allotment
9. Criminal Protection Associate
10. Drug Cartel
11. Uncooperative Pigeon Slave
12. Behavior Modification Wagon
13. Re-education & Reprogramming
14. Trafficking Sales (& Service! ☺)™ Abduction
15. Pole-dancing Portfolio
16. Vampire Insurance Professionals

"Well, I'm prepping for a trip to the UAE[17] to meet with some people about getting my PHD,[18] so I have to get my CV[19] done."

"Yep, you don't want to wind up with an STD,[20] and you might even have to deal with an HIV[21] issue!"

"Right, that's definitely no fun. Last time, my girlfriend had to go see her MD[22] for some kind of issue with her IUD[23], but he fed her a whole bunch of BS,[24] so she wasn't feeling like herself for days.[25] But anyway, tonight I'm in the mood for a little T&A,[26] so I'm looking forward to a steamy, intimate night with my GF.[27] Later!"

Teacher: Umm, thank you for the essay, but that's not exactly what labor unions do, Timmy.

Union boss (*brandishing baseball bat*):[28] Are you callin' us weak, lady?

---

17. Uncertified Association of Enemists
18. Prepaid Hour with 9-year-old Dubai prostitute
19. Chlamydia Vaccine
20. Surprise! Twin Daughters
21. Human Import (& Export! ☺)™ Vendor
22. Menstruation Director
23. Incontinence Undergarment Denial
24. Botulism Sundae
25. weeks
26. *Trugenderis ambiguus*
27. Grandfather
28. This is in fact what labor unions do.

- fin -